Wilbie
finds
a friend

For Theo

MYRIAD BOOKS LIMITED
35 Bishopsthorpe Road, London SE26 4PA

First published in 2004 by
PICCADILLY PRESS LIMITED
5 Castle Road, London NW1 8PR
www.piccadillypress.co.uk

Text and illustrations copyright © Sally Chambers 2004

ISBN 1 905606 93 1
EAN 9 781905 606 931

Text designed by Louise Millar

Printed in China

Wilbie
finds
a friend

Sally
Chambers

MYRIAD BOOKS LIMITED

It was the beginning of the holidays
and Wilbie was very excited.
He was going to play football.
He was going to play it all the time.

Wilbie loved playing football,
    but there was one problem . . .

His garden was small and the
ball kept going over the fence.
It happened all the time.
But somehow the ball always came back ...

On Monday he headed it over the fence just before lunch.
But by the time he had eaten his sandwiches the ball was back.

On Tuesday he kicked it over the fence just before dinner.
But by the time he had eaten his cake the ball was back.

On Wednesday he booted the ball over the fence just before bedtime.

And the next day when he woke up, there it was, on the lawn, just as before. He never thought about it — it just came back.

It was Thursday and Wilbie's friend
Harry was coming to play.
They rushed out into the
garden with the football.

But within a short time,
Wilbie had kicked the
ball over the fence.

"Never mind," he told Harry. "Let's get a drink and by the time we have finished it, the ball will be back on the grass."

But when they came back the ball wasn't on the grass.

They waited for a little while, but the ball didn't come back.

So they waited a little longer . . .

But still it didn't
come back.

They waited impatiently all morning.

Finally, Wilbie decided
he would look over
the fence.

The garden next door was
very overgrown. There was a rusty
old bike, a broken greenhouse,
a dustbin and lots and lots of flower pots.
But there was no sign of the ball.

"My ball hasn't come back," Wilbie told his mum.
"Can you go and get it for me?"

"We'll go together," she said, "but I think you should say
thank you for all the times your ball has been returned.
Mr Appleby is quite old and he may not be well."

Wilbie was
not very happy.
He thought old
people were boring.
They never did anything
except sit around and talk.

After a while, the door opened.
Wilbie and Harry couldn't believe their eyes.
The inside of the house was amazing.

Everywhere they looked there were football things.
Pictures, photos, trophies, cups, shirts, flags –
everything you could think of to do with football.

"Sorry I didn't return your ball," Mr Appleby said, "but I've not been too well today. I've been sitting looking at some of my old photos. Would you like to have a look?"

Mr Appleby had been a football fan since he was a boy.
He had collected everything he could about
football – just like Wilbie.

Wilbie was fascinated.
They spent ages looking
at all sorts of things – photos . . .

scrapbooks . . .

scarves . . .

trophies . . .

match programmes, posters . . .

There was even an old football.
"Wow! Did you really play with that?" said Wilbie. "It's so heavy." Wilbie couldn't believe his eyes.

Finally it was time for Wilbie and Harry to go home.
"Can we come again, please?" asked Wilbie.
"Well, I don't know, you'll have to ask your mum, but I'm sure you will need to come back for your ball now and again."

From then on whenever Wilbie kicked the ball over the fence, he didn't mind going to ask for it back.

In fact, sometimes he did it on purpose just so he could go and see Mr Appleby and hear some more of his stories.

Soon it was time to start school again. On Friday, everyone took turns to talk about their holidays.

Wilbie told the class about
Mr Appleby. Everyone listened in silence.
And when Wilbie finished, they all clapped very loudly.

Mr Appleby had even lent him his football
to show the class. Everyone took turns to hold it.

Wilbie decided he would call in on
Mr Appleby on his way home. He was
very proud of himself and his new friend.

Older people weren't boring after all.
In fact they have fantastic stories to tell. If you listen.